Princess T

Builds a Snowman

WRITTEN BY Kelly Greenawalt

ILLUSTRATED BY Amariah Rauscher

Cartwheel Books

An imprint of Scholastic Inc.

New York

I climb out of my cozy bed.
I run to my window.
Everything I see is white.
Look at that fluffy snow!

I wake up my brother, Ty.
We want to go and play.

First, we must bundle up.
It's very cold today.

I want to build a snowman.
I place three snowballs on the ground.

Ty and Noodles want to help.
We roll them round and round.

We stack up our snowman.
We gather our supplies.

I give him two stick arms.
Ty adds the mouth and eyes.

He looks very chilly.
We put on his warm clothes.
Something is missing!
Our snowman needs a nose.

Our friends are going sledding.
We want to do that, too.
But our snowman might get lonely.
I know just what to do.

We need rainbow magic.
My curls glisten and glow.
Our snowman starts to sparkle.
Then he smiles and says, "Hello!"

We all hop on the sled.
We whiz and we whirl.
We speed past our friends.
We swish and we swirl.

Next, we put on our skates.
We glide and we spin.
Then we play a game!
Our snowman helps us win.

GOAL

It is time to go home.
We have to say goodbye.
Our snowman looks lonely,
and then he starts to cry.

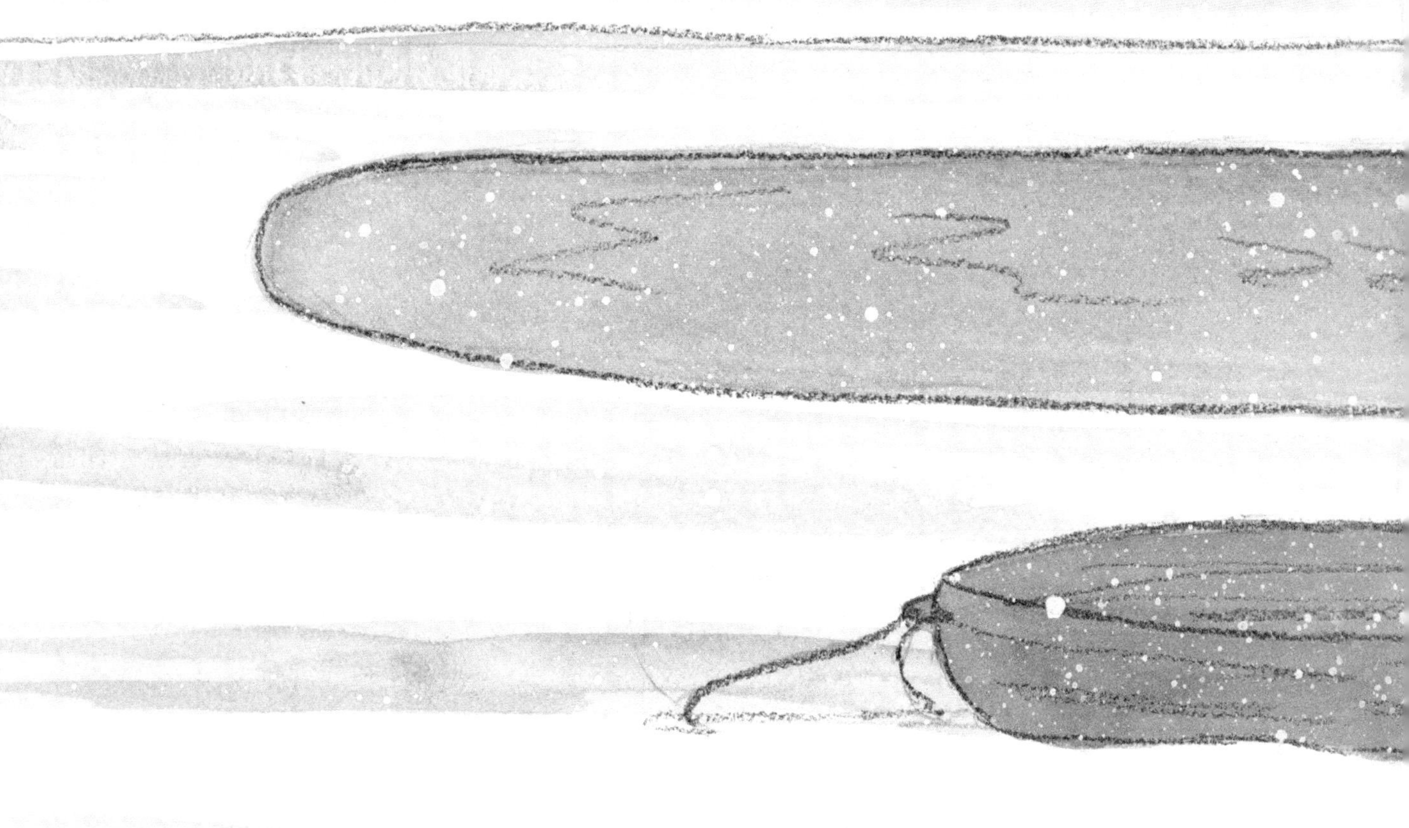

I have a great idea!
My magic curls shine bright.
I make him a new friend.
They glide and spin all night.

To my beautiful mother, I love you more. –K.G.

For Jalen and Junia –A.R.

 Published by Scholastic Inc., *Publishers since 1920.* SCHOLASTIC, CARTWHEEL BOOKS, and associated logos are trademarks and/or registered trademarks of Scholastic Inc. • Library of Congress Cataloging-in-Publication Data available • ISBN 978-1-338-83091-0
10 9 8 7 6 5 4 3 2 1 24 25 26 27 28 • Printed in the U.S.A. 40 • First edition, October 2024 • The text type was set in Palatino. The display type was set in KG Be Still and Know. • The illustrations were created using watercolor and charcoal.
Designed by Rae Crawford